THE STATE OF KANSAS

THE STATE OF KANSAS

short (and very short) fictions by

JULIANNA SPALLHOLZ

Julianna Spallholz, The State of Kansas
© 2012 Julianna Spallholz

First edition, January 2012
ISBN-13: 9780982359440
Printed and bound in the USA.
Library of Congress Control Number: 2011930271

Cover design by Jennifer Whittingham.
Illustrations on pages 1, 43, 55, and 57 by Geralee Hall.
Illustrations on pages 22, 73, 75, and 80 by Nòah Saterstrom.

for Mom, Dad, Drue, Scott, and Phineas

Contents

The State
of
Kansas

BRICKS

I have been welcomed into homes I should not have been welcomed into. I have admired ceiling fixtures and well-slung cloths and have taken the wine and the most comfortable chairs of my hosts. I have let myself into their medicine cabinets. I have crossed my legs on the edges of their desks and have coveted their sparkling kitchen floors. I have touched things I probably should not have touched. I have this long strand of beads that, when hanging over my finger, rests nicely on the ground. I once lost that strand of beads and then I found it. I often sit on my fire escape and look at the bricks of my tall building and then I look at them closely and closely and closely. I am trying to understand my relationship with the bricks. I figure that if I can do that then I could do something else and then maybe something else and then maybe if I'm lucky something else.

Pretend

Pretend that the bathroom floor needs scrubbing. Pretend that the furniture needs to be rearranged. Pretend to examine the leaves of the ivy or the vine or whatever it is. Pretend there are brown spots and pretend to be concerned. Pretend to like the mustard wallpaper that was pasted on by the tenant before. Pretend to look forward to sitcoms. Pretend to look forward to anything. Pretend to plan a dinner party. Pretend to throw it. Pretend to be interested in the Mapplethorpe book from the library. Talk about it to friends. Pretend to look for kick boxing classes in the paper. Pretend to get dressed in the morning and go to work. Pretend to give a shit about work. Pretend to walk tall and pretend to wiggle a little bit when passing men on the street. Pretend not to. Pretend the new brown boots don't hurt. Pretend nothing does. Get excited about Christmas. Get excited about sex. Dream about New York City and Vermont and Paris. Want to get married. Absolutely do not want to get married. Pretend not to have already named the kids. Two boys and a girl. Pretend to want an artistic life. Pretend to have one. Use words like brilliant and phenomenal. Pretend to know how to spell phenomenal on the first try. Know when to call movies films. Pretend not to miss home. Pretend to know where that is anymore. Pretend to feel okay about wearing slippers. Pretend not to be somewhat jealous of people on Paxil. Pretend to be sometimes attracted to women. Pretend not to be. Pretend to quit smoking. Pretend cigarettes don't look kinda cool. Pretend not to be psyched about having big breasts. Pretend to not be embarrassed when buying condoms and tampons. Pretend to save money for a trip to the southwest. Think the southwest is impressive. Talk casually about Manhattan. Talk disgustedly about the government. Pretend to listen to NPR and pretend to understand anything about anything. Pretend to be fine with the break-up. Pretend not to be a cheat. Pretend to know how to love and be loved. Pretend not to probably need therapy. Pretend to need therapy. Pretend to sweep the bedroom floor. Pretend it is clean.

THE BUG

There was a bug in the corner of her kitchen. It was up near the ceiling, above the sink and next to the window. The girl noticed it one morning when coming out of the shower. She was wrapped in a red towel and in a hurry, getting ready for work. She thought about killing it. She thought about climbing up on a stool or propping herself on the counter and smashing it with a tissue. But she took a step closer and saw that the bug was a big bug. She did not want to get her fingers that close. Also, the bug might fall awkwardly and touch her skin, exposed as she was in only a towel. The girl decided to get dressed first.

She went into the bedroom and chose pants and a shirt. She put them on and looked in the mirror. The shirt was not fresh and she saw that there was a smear across the breast. She pulled the shirt off and put on another one. It was a bit wrinkled, but good enough. She walked back to the bathroom. On the way, she looked at the bug again. She could not tell if it had moved. She did not want to kill it without shoes on. But the bathroom was closer now than the bedroom where the shoes were, so she went inside and dried her hair. She brushed her teeth. She put on make-up and chose a pair of earrings, hanging silver with a garnet stone. A hair had fallen from her head and landed on the edge of the bathroom sink. She washed it down with a handful of water.

The girl went back into the kitchen. She still did not know if the bug had moved, but from where she stood she could see more of its body. She considered smashing the bug with the bristles of the broom, but she was hungry and thought she should eat breakfast first. She pulled the toaster from the cabinet and the bread from the refrigerator. When the toast was done, she spread it with butter. She took milk from the refrigerator and checked the expiration date. It was on its last day and so she sniffed it. It smelled fine, and the girl poured herself a cup of coffee. She picked up her plate of toast and her mug and went toward the table.

The girl glanced up at the corner where the bug was. At first she could not see it and felt a vague sense of panic. But no, there it was, just to the left of where she was looking. It still had not moved. She was sure of it. She sat down at the table and ate her toast and drank her coffee slowly because it was hot. She had to get up once from the table to retrieve a paper napkin because her fingers were sticky. She licked them first before wiping them off. The girl looked over her phone bill, which was thick and expensive. It made her feel nervous and she put it aside, under a basket, out of sight until later.

She reread a letter she had received in the mail a few weeks before. The letter was on white paper and had been written in black ink. It had come in a yellow envelope, which was ripped across the top. The handwriting was messy but legible and the words were comprised of both lower and uppercase letters. The girl had read once, in article about handwriting analysis, that a person who includes uppercase letters in the middle of a word has something to hide. This thought made her for a moment feel angry and desperate, but, the girl remembered, she herself was in the habit of making uppercase Rs and Ns in the middle of words. This did not make her feel better. Instead, the girl wondered what it was that she herself was hiding.

When she was done rereading the letter, the girl looked up at the bug. From across the room it looked just like a smudge of dirt or a gathering of dust. It looked like nothing at all. She put on her shoes and went to work.

When the girl returned home that afternoon, she kicked her shoes off and checked her messages. There was a message from her mother, who was just checking in. There was a message from her college roommate, too, who was also checking in. She deleted both these messages, took a beer from the refrigerator, and sat down at the kitchen table. She pulled the pages of her phone bill out from beneath the basket. She ran her eyes down the list of calls she had made. She wondered if there was a mistake. She could not believe there were so many. She wondered how she would afford it. She thought about money and how it feels wasted, how she could not remember most of the calls, how they all seemed like one call, how they had not gotten her anywhere.

The girl placed the phone bill back under the basket and sipped on her beer until it was almost gone. She remembered the bug and looked up. She was positive that it still had not moved. It looked rounder to her than it had before, as if it had collected dust in just one afternoon.

The girl took a final sip and picked up the letter. She reread only phrases of it this time, and she noticed that the words were beginning to feel meaningless and predictable. She tried to read the letter again from the beginning, as if she had never read it before. She thought for a moment that she felt something new, something she hadn't felt previously from the letter, but the sensation left her quickly. She looked at her own name, written out on top. There were three uppercase letters within it. They stood out to her, became garish and insulting. She held the letter in her hand and looked back up at the bug. The longer she looked at it, the darker and dirtier it appeared against the white kitchen walls and ceiling. She was certain that it had not moved. She decided that the bug was already dead. She wondered how long it had been there before she noticed, hanging in the corner, obvious like that.

HOME

We argued about what *home* is. I got the dictionary. I looked up *home*. I read the definitions out loud. One. The place where one resides. Two. A house. Three. A customary environment; habitat. Four. You rolled your eyes. Wait, I said. Four. A place of origin. Five. To the center or heart of something; deeply. Six. Having an easy competence and familiarity. I put the dictionary down. I told you, I said. You opened your mouth but then you closed it again.

We reside in a house in an environment that is not our place of origin, and though we are accustomed to an easy competence and familiarity, we know that we have not gotten to the center or to the heart of something, deeply.

BRUSHING

In the morning when the young woman goes to brush her teeth, she discovers that the old bathroom sink is stopped up, a pool of water thick with hair and dust in the basin. She paints the toothbrush bristles with blue paste and walks toward the window.

The young man is outside leaning over the open hood of his car, which has, he says, been leaking oil for the last week. He is wearing a white t-shirt. The young woman can see his belly where the sun shines behind him. She tries to open the window but it is stuck. She places her toothbrush handle in her mouth like a rose, and repositions her palms on the windowsill. She pushes harder. Still it does not open. She takes her toothbrush out of her mouth and raps her knuckles on the glass. The young man does not look up. The young woman raps again, and he stands. She waves at him. He waits for her to speak. She tries to make her voice thick and strong, to be heard.

"I need to brush my teeth," she says, and smiles.

His face tightens and appears irritated. He thrusts his head forward. He did not hear her. She speaks louder.

"I need to brush my teeth," she says. She holds up her toothbrush and points to it.

"Oh," he says. "Do it in the kitchen sink." His voice sounds bottled and far away.

The young woman turns and walks to the kitchen. She stands before the kitchen sink. It is full of dishes, precariously piled glasses, bowls with floating cereal O's, half drunk mugs of coffee. She pinches her nostrils against the stench and moves a pile aside. The drain is filled with ancient spaghetti and peas. She considers removing them but then imagines how it would feel between her fingers.

She walks back to the window.

She raps on the glass. The young man looks up. "What?" he says rudely.

"The sink is full of dishes," the young woman says and purses her lips.

"What?" he says again, his forehead wrinkly and his mouth twisted.

"The sink is full of dishes!" she yells.

He lights a cigarette and blows out the smoke. "So do it in the bathtub," he says.

She turns and walks back to the bathroom.

Sitting on the edge of the tub, the young woman reaches out and cranks the coldwater handle. The water comes out rusty at first. It loosens a clump of hair from the drain, hers mixed with his, which floats around and then settles. She puts her brush under the stream and then into her mouth. The water tastes funny, almost dry. She has always considered bathtub water to be inferior to sink water, but with some things you just have to make do.

Your Maid in Real Life

I had a dream that you were fucking your maid. In real life you don't have a maid, but in my dream your maid was terribly in love with you and you were taking her for a ride. I knew that you would break the heart of your maid.

Your maid was older, short, and rather plump, and her teeth had gaping spaces. I walked by a room and you were in there dancing with your maid, spinning and laughing amidst the laundry, white billowing sheets everywhere. Your wife was at work. You were making your maid's day.

Your maid was very stupid to think that maybe you were really in love. Your maid was very stupid to think that maybe you wouldn't kick her to the curb.

I kind of felt sorry for your maid and I kind of hated her. I stood with your maid in an alley while she spoke passionately about you, her neck craned, her arms suddenly and gracefully athletic, her hands tensed, poised, invigorated. I didn't correct her. I understood. The streetlights shone down on us. The cobblestones were romantically wet. Your maid had stars in her lonely eyes. Your maid felt like a girl again. Your maid had so much hope.

It wouldn't be very long before your wife came home from work. It wouldn't be very long before your maid was reminded that her actual job was to clean the pubic hair off your bathroom floor.

Your poor stupid maid.

I envied her. I remembered being that stupid, how perfect it was, all billowing white dream sheets and dancing, you, the feeling of believing that every beautiful impossible thing could be real.

THE BODY

The body is not perfect but it could be. The body remembers boys on the school bus making fun of its nose and teeth. The body knows not to smoke but it smokes anyway. The body scratches its head too hard and gets blood beneath its fingernails. The body has long legs but notices spider veins. The body spent some time not eating and then some time in baggy clothes. The body is vegetarian but likes the smell of ham. The body does not like to run. The body drinks too much. The body gets headaches often and earaches in the spring. The body has been told that it is tense. The body has been told that it is tall. The body has been told that it is graceful but also that it moves like some strange animal. The body didn't know how to take that. The body is scarred where its moles have been taken. The body has never broken a bone or been stung by a bee. The body may be allergic to bees, it doesn't know. The body suffers from some of its own likes. The body sleeps too much or not enough. The body once fell down stone stairs in wooden shoes. The body once sat too long in the sun and became blistered. The body picks its nose. The body once slipped with a knife and almost lost its pinky. The body used to fall asleep in the Volvo and be carried in. The body has odd visions of sharp things in its eyes and of jumping when it shouldn't jump. The body's toenails need to be cut and re-painted. The body shivers when someone plays with its hair. The body has memorized smells. The body does not know how to really play an instrument but recalls the flute a little. It sings. The body did not orgasm until it was twenty years old. The body has experienced a variety of sex and some of it was bad and some very good, and some the body thought was good was bad and vice versa. The body responds well to yellow. The body cries and also laughs quite easily and in both cases, the body's face gets rather pink. The body took its time growing breasts but it managed. The body used to like swings and probably still does. The body likes to put its fingers into containers that hold a lot of the same thing, like M&M's or water. The body imagines doing things it does not actually do, like screaming and being upside down. The body does not like to lie still unless it is allowed to go to sleep. The body gets ravenously hungry and feels as if it will faint. The body has fainted for real three times, two of the times as a game, one of the times by not eating. Being scared by something real or by something imagined makes the body dizzy.

BILLY GLOCK

One night after dinner my father feels pains in his chest. My mother calls the paramedics. My father sits on the couch with his head bowed, his right hand grabbing his left shoulder. I go to the bathroom.

The paramedics come. One of the paramedics is Billy Glock from elementary school.

Billy Glock from elementary school! By God. I haven't thought about Billy Glock in ages. In second grade Billy Glock threw up on my green science folder!

I watch Billy Glock from elementary school kneel in front of my father. I hear Billy Glock from elementary school speak to my father with soothing authority.

Billy Glock from elementary school is the boss paramedic. The other paramedics just kind of hang around.

I see Billy Glock from elementary school using medical tools on my father. The red lights from the ambulance come in through the living room windows and bounce around on my father's face.

I got better grades than Billy Glock.

I remember that Billy Glock had diabetes. When it was Billy Glock's birthday all the kids got regular Popsicles and Billy Glock got a special Popsicle that he had to eat sitting down with a fork and plate.

Who would have known, in second grade, when Billy Glock stole my eraser, that Billy Glock would one day be in my parents' living room, monitoring my father's heart, while I wander around the rug chewing on my fingers like some helpless chump.

My father looks scared.

I wonder if this is the day that will be the day when I will have to start living the rest of my life without my father. I wonder what Billy Glock thinks of me now, if he thinks I am pretty.

I am scared that my father will die.

Billy Glock, please save my father.

Room

I rescue cats from a burning building. There are dozens of cats and I rescue every single one of them. When I am done rescuing the cats I am exhausted and I smell like fire. I have done all I can do and I have done it well. The man I am in love with thinks that I am a hero. He takes me to a beautiful old room with old furniture and many dripping candles and velvet curtains and peeling paint. He takes care of me while I recuperate, which doesn't take that long. It is clear to him then how terrific I am and how much he loves me. We make love in the room for seven days.

A Terrible Wait

The young man and the young woman boarded a subway train that was headed to the borough of New York City where they made their home. The way the young man and the young woman made their home was by sleeping, showering and storing their belongings in an apartment they paid rent on each month. At the last stop before the subway train was to leave the island, a man boarded the subway train and sat in the seat across from the young man and the young woman.

The man had a parcel in his hands. He placed the parcel on his lap. The parcel was a bath towel wrapped around whatever was inside. The bath towel was held closed by rubber bands. The man removed the rubber bands from the bath towel and removed what was inside. What was inside was a large knife.

As the subway train entered the part of the tunnel that ran beneath the river, the man flicked the blade of the large knife around on his palms and on the thighs of his jeans. He tested the edge of the large knife with his thumb. He stared strangely at the passengers on the subway train. He stared at the young man and he stared at the young woman. The young man and the young woman and the other passengers on the subway train waited a terrible wait to see what would happen.

When the subway train approached the first stop in the borough where the young man and the young woman made their home, the man wrapped the butcher knife back up in its bath towel and replaced the rubber bands. The man took his parcel and got off the subway train. The young man and the young woman were free to return to the apartment in the borough of New York City where they made their home.

In telling the story for weeks, months and years after, the young woman would call the knife a butcher knife with emphasis on the word butcher, but she was secretly never sure what made a knife butcher or not. The young man never pointed this out and the young woman was silently appreciative.

MY BOYFRIEND

My boyfriend is a vampire, which is good because we live in a dark and dangerous city and I need the protection. I am proud of my vampire boyfriend, proud of his black leather outfit and slick hairdo. He is so much worldlier than I, I who wear jeans and sweatshirts and cotton underwear and socks and worry about things like money. My boyfriend has a funny way of talking. His vampire accent makes it hard for me to understand the things he says. I am often unsure whether the things my boyfriend says are nice things or mean vampire things, so I choose to believe that the things he says are nice. It makes everything a little easier for both of us. When we walk along the street together we get strange looks due to my boyfriend's very pale skin and unique way of staring at people, but this only makes me squeeze his chilly hand tighter. That my boyfriend is a vampire is not his fault after all, because of the situation several years ago with the silly careless princess and her angry father and the bat and the ring of fire and the curse, blah blah. Yes my boyfriend may turn on me, yes my boyfriend may grab me roughly by the shoulders, yes my boyfriend may shove me up against a wall, yes my boyfriend may bend me backward forcefully and denounce my living flesh and yank my hair and instill fear in me, yes my boyfriend may open his mouth, yes my boyfriend's eyes may turn yellow, yes my boyfriend may thrust his pointy teeth forward and pierce my skin and my vein and drink from me until there is nothing left and I am dead or until there is just barely something left at which point yes my boyfriend may leave me to die, but believe me when I say that I am willing to take this risk because I love my boyfriend and it keeps our sex life edgy.

ROOF

I walk into the kitchen of my apartment. The window has been left open. I climb through the window to the roof. Something is terribly wrong. Oh God, where is my cat? I already know and now it is my time to see it. I walk to the edge of the roof. I look down. My cat is lying dead on the cement far below. I kneel and grip the edge of the roof. I yell his name and I yell his name. Such terror, such grief. My little black and white cat, my baby. No! No! I loved him and it was my job to protect him. We live in this stupid city. Now he is dead and alone. It is my fault.

poor cat

Dog

She takes the Labrador retriever to the park in the late evening. She and the Labrador retriever enter the park. She hears a high-pitched whistling screaming sound. She also hears cheering. She looks up the hill in the park. There is a cluster of men standing near a tree. There is a dog hanging by its mouth from a limb of the tree. The dog is a pit bull terrier. The pit bull terrier is clenching the limb of the tree in its mouth. The pit bull terrier is screaming. The men are cheering. The pit bull terrier will not let go of the limb of the tree until the men tell it to let go. The men will not tell it to let go. She is afraid of the men and she is afraid of the pit bull terrier. The pit bull terrier will defend the men who will not tell it to let go. She and the Labrador retriever leave the park.

MEN

She goes with her boyfriend to visit her boyfriend's brother. Her boyfriend's brother lives in a bad part of town. His apartment is above a vacuum shop. Her boyfriend's brother has no shirt on. There are other men there. They have no shirts on. It is the middle of the day. Her boyfriend's brother wears a cowboy hat. He is sitting in a ripped armchair. He and the other men are watching *The Last of the Mohicans*. It is hot in the apartment. There is garbage. There is beer in cans. She sits on her boyfriend's brother's couch. There is a spider crawling on the wall. Her boyfriend's brother sees the spider and gets up from the armchair. He catches the spider in his hand. He holds the spider by its leg and dangles the spider in front of her face. She puts her hand up to block the spider. The other men snicker. Her boyfriend says nothing. Her boyfriend's brother puts the spider on a table. He gets a large hunting knife and holds the spider down. The spider wriggles. He uses the hunting knife to cut off each of the spider's legs. He pauses between each leg. He laughs and sweats. The other men cheer him on. It takes a long time. The spider dies.

Her boyfriend's brother sits back down in the armchair. They watch *The Last of the Mohicans*. Her boyfriend's brother gets up from the armchair. He leaves the room. He comes back holding a rifle. He kneels on the floor in front of the couch where she sits. He does things with the rifle. He puts the rifle on his shoulder and turns so that the rifle is pointing at her face. It is hot in the apartment. Everything is tight and silent. She puts her hand up to block the rifle. Please take the gun away from my face, she says. He laughs and sweats. Some of the other men snicker. Please take the gun away from my face, she says. He laughs and sweats. She looks at him over the top of the rifle. She can see his eyes. One of the other men says Enough. He takes the gun away from her face.

Hero

The week after the flood, I went to the diner. The streets were sloshy and there was stinking devastation everywhere, but things were starting to look up. Small groups of men were doing modest demolition work and drinking cold beers. I saw the woman from down the street walking her one surviving dog.

I ordered eggs and potatoes and toast and orange juice. I was very hungry and I had a little money. Also they were playing my second favorite song. Even the usually grumpy waitress seemed chipper.

"Some flood," she said.

"Yes," I said.

She poured my coffee.

I was only halfway through my delicious meal when you walked in. I immediately lost my appetite and pushed my plate away. I hadn't seen you in at least ten days. You had been busy rescuing the neighborhood's ancestral furniture and treed kittens. You said hello to the only other two occupied tables, but didn't notice me until you were served your tall glass of whole milk, which you then raised at me from a few booths down.

"How's things," you said loudly.

"Oh fine," I said. "I had to bail the living room out all by myself, the kitchen ceiling caved in, and the iguana almost drowned. You?"

"Busy," you said.

"I'll bet," I said. "By the way, your box of stuff got ruined."

You swallowed your milk hard and stared at me.

"My box of stuff?" you said.

I nodded.

"I thought I told you to put my box of stuff on the high shelf," you said.

I shrugged. "I took it down."

You planted your glass of milk on the table and turned your head regretfully to the side. You breathed deeply.

"I loved that goddamn box of stuff," you said.

"I know," I said. "And I loved you. C'est la vie."

You turned to look at me again. "What's that supposed to mean?"

"Exactly what you think it means," I said. "Nothing."

We had met at the public pool. You liked how I looked in my bathing suit and I watched you save a little kid by giving him mouth-to-mouth. His mother had been overjoyed. Obviously. We went out for beers. You were broke and had a running bar tab of three months' worth, and so you moved in with me. It was supposed to be temporary, but you were kind to your grandma, who you went to see every Sunday, so I let it go on until you started bringing drunk cops and firefighters to the house in the middle of the night and I would have to get out of bed and make them coffee and bacon. I'm a vegetarian and it pissed me off. You watched a lot of TV and ate a bunch of food, which I paid for. Nothing was ever going to get better and the best I could hope for was back to normal, so, begrudgingly, I kicked you out. You had such a nice ass.

The waitress brought you your sausage and biscuits with gravy. She wiped her hands on her apron. She thanked you for getting her husband down off the roof and told you that your breakfast was on the house. Nobody got it but me.

"I do what I can," you said, which, I thought, was a reasonable response.

On the way home things were looking all right. Kids had taken their sneakers off and were stomping mud at each other in the playground. Elderly people were being wheeled back into the retirement home and the hobos who hang out in front of the community theater were drinking again on their regular benches. Sometimes you do some good work. I was sure that the swampy stench that lingered everywhere would last for a while more, but I didn't suppose there was much to be done about that. We would all just have to wait it out.

Simple

In an effort to make it simple, she threw out her furniture. She threw out her jewelry and her decorations and her photographs. But still it was not simple. She threw out her shoes. She threw out her soap. She threw out her clothes. But still it was not simple. She threw out her car. She threw out her food. She threw out her apartment. But still it was not simple. She threw out her money. And then she was dirty and cold and hungry and broke. But still it was not simple. She threw out her language. She threw out simple. But still it was not.

THE STATE OF KANSAS

I am learning the states, said the girl's mother. I recite the states to myself when I am trying to get to sleep. I used to do the alphabet backward but it became too easy. So now I do the states.

I know the states in alphabetical order, said the girl. But I do not know where the states go.

I am learning where the states go, said the girl's mother. I have several copies of a blank map to test myself. I fill in the states by heart. Yesterday I got all the states but one. The state I forgot was the state of Kansas.

The state of Kansas, said the girl. There are many states I would forget but I do not think I would forget the state of Kansas.

Well *I* forgot the state of Kansas, said the girl's mother. And I'll bet you would forget the state of Kansas too. The states in the middle are a bitch.

The states in the middle *are* a bitch, said the girl.

Yes, said the girl's mother. A bitch. Have you ever noticed how small the states are in the east and how big the states are in the west?

I *have* noticed that, said the girl.

And how straight the states are in the west and how jagged the states are in the east?

Very jagged, said the girl.

Until last week, I couldn't keep those jagged states straight! said the girl's mother.

I don't think *I* could keep those jagged states straight, said the girl.

Picture New York, said the girl's mother.

The girl pictured New York.

Now picture Maine, said the girl's mother.

I cannot picture Maine, said the girl.

Maine is the state in the corner, said the girl's mother.

The girl pictured Maine.

Now remember that everything I am about to say is between New York and Maine, said the girl's mother. Vermont, New Hampshire, Connecticut, Massachusetts, and the itty bitty state of Rhode Island.

I knew that the state of Rhode Island was itty bitty, said the girl.

Simply knowing the size won't do you much good, said the girl's mother. Can you go down the coast?

East coast or west coast? said the girl.

East coast, said the girl's mother.

I think I can go down the coast, said the girl.

Do you think or do you know? said the girl's mother.

The girl shut her eyes. New Jersey Delaware Maryland Virginia, said the girl.

Keep going down, said the girl's mother.

North Carolina South Carolina, said the girl.

Don't forget the state before the state of Florida, said the girl's mother.

The state of Georgia? said the girl.

The state of Georgia! said the girl's mother.

The state of Georgia was founded by James Oglethorpe, said the girl.

Impressive, said the girl's mother.

Maybe *I* could learn the states, said the girl. Then I could do the rest of the continent and then the whole hemisphere. Hell, maybe I could do the world!

Let us not get ahead of ourselves, said the girl's mother. For now we'll just stick to the states.

ARIZONA
(for Ruby Jets)

I had recently moved to southern Arizona and I went to a big party and drank lots of whiskey. By the end of the big party I felt embarrassed and angry and like a certain person was making great upward strides in the business of breaking my heart. I brought my friend, who also drank lots of whiskey, home with me. My friend and I went to the kitchen and drank more whiskey. I lost my temper and yelled and kicked the kitchen cabinet. I was wearing fierce boots. I kicked the kitchen cabinet lots of times. My friend fell off his chair. He was on the floor. Take that, Cabinet! I kicked the shit out of that cabinet.

Adult Matters

I know that I started it by stomping on your foot but you should not have chased after me with that bright red chair. It was frightening for all the little children who do not understand such adult matters.

Neighborhood

They have closed off the underpass for rebuilding. Everyone is mad. Now we must go around, climb over the tracks. There have been accidents: homeless people, drunk people, friends. Homeless drunk friends. One bad one in particular. He lived. It was a miracle. The neighborhood was very concerned, which is good, which says something good about our neighborhood.

The neighbors across the street have a pit bull terrier that gets loose and comes over and terrorizes my cats. I scream for help. I scream and scream. I scream obscenities. The neighbors do nothing. They watch from their porch. Eventually I am triumphant. My cats are unharmed. I drag the pit bull terrier back across the street and put it angrily behind the neighbors' fence. I look angrily at the neighbors on their porch. I do not speak Spanish and the neighbors do not speak English, except the children, three little girls who told me I was pretty once when I went outside in my nightgown to take out the trash. They are also very pretty.

The 24-hour bar and diner has been closed for three days because of plumbing problems. There is a terrible smell. We walk by or ride by on our bikes and we look sideways at the bar and diner. No one says anything but we feel rather uncomfortable. We don't know where to drink or to eat eggs together. We are out of sorts.

They are tearing down a building. We think that they should not tear it down. It is an old building, very beautiful. We don't know what they will build there. Probably something boring. We talk about it on the sidewalk and are mad. We have not been to any meetings. We should go to meetings. We should not have to go to any meetings. Jesus. They should know enough to not just tear it down.

A friend down the street built a chicken coop in his backyard. He got twenty-five chickens. A neighbor complained. The city intervened. Now he has to kill half the chickens. He does it with the help of other neighbors. They spend the day wringing the necks of chickens. They are unskilled. While it is happening, the rest of us go to each others' houses and speak quietly, over coffee. We discuss death and responsibility and the lives of animals.

We are up all night drinking and then we decide to drive out to nature. We climb up on a rock. We watch the sunset. It is beautiful, amazing. This is why we live here, says one of us, and I think it's embarrassing. I do not think we need to discuss how small we are.

Business Idea

My friends come up with a business idea. For days I hear them talk about their business idea. They make plans about their business idea. They draw an outline for their business idea. They sit at the kitchen table. They use fine point black markers. They become excitable. They draft a budget for their business idea. They use imaginary money. Their business idea will not work. After several days they stop talking about their business idea. They never talk about their business idea again. I am relieved.

A Brief Introduction to Downtown Tucson, Arizona

Heat

It gets so hot here in the summer that people drive their cars wearing oven mitts. It is difficult to touch anything made of metal. The trees provide little shade. You can feel heat from buildings and from the road. The air itself is hot and the breeze is also hot. Sometimes there are dust storms that come down the street in house-sized tornadoes and sound like an approaching herd of big animals. The dust storms collect branches and chairs and garbage cans and dump them somewhere else.

Water

It is ill advised to walk very far without water. Water in bottles gets warm very quickly. Coldwater faucets produce warm water. There used to be a river but now there is no river or lake or stream or pond or creek or brook or puddle. The only water is what falls from the sky. Monsoon comes in mid-summer. Each day in late afternoon there are dark clouds and the sky gets black and yellow and red and heavy and everyone goes outside and looks at the sky and waits for rain. The storms are severe. Palm trees bend and the streets flood. Often it is impossible to drive through the flooded areas. Everyone loves monsoon. When it rains the air smells like creosote, which smells like soft brown sweet dirt musk.

Architecture

There are three skyscrapers in the business section, which stretches about three blocks, and in midday the area is bustling, almost like a big city. But mostly there are short old adobe buildings painted with bright colors, which are peoples' houses. Many buildings also display mural work and many still have faded old painted signs of businesses like "Mercado" and "La Tortillaria." There are dusty colorful old cars and trucks resting on the sides of the roads.

Jobs

Some downtowners work at the little market, some work at the nicer restaurants, and some work at the bike shop. There are some banks and other offices. You could work at the University or at Raytheon, which is a place where they make weapons. A lot of people seem like they don't have jobs, or like they have jobs that don't take up too much time. You can live well on very little here. No one cares if you're broke.

Fashion

Lots of woman hipsters wear forties or fifties vintage dresses. Lots of men wear fancy pants, shirts, and shoes from thrift stores. A lot of people go totally ragamuffin and some go cowboy. There are a lot of tattoos, dyed hair, and ironic mustaches.

Food

There are several cheap restaurants, and some middle, and a few upscale. The best Mexican is on the south side. There is one 24-hour diner. There is one international market and one organic co-op.

Booze

Everyone drinks. There are always people you know in bars to drink with at all times of day and night. Even if you're broke you can get drunk. $1 PBRs at Che's, $1.50 Schlitz at Congress, $1 High Life at the Grill. At the District you can get a High Life and a whiskey for something like $4. Sometimes you end up getting drunk without meaning to. Entire days go by in bars. Entire weeks and months.

Plants

Prickly pear cactus grows all over the place. It is very hearty. If you snap a pad off of one and stick it in the dirt, a new cactus will grow. People also plant barrel cactus and sometimes saguaro. Bougainvillea is a common vine flower. Its blossoms are bright pink and very striking. Some other flowers are Mexican Hat and Desert Poppy. Mesquite trees and Palo Verde trees are everywhere. So are palm trees, but they are not native. There is very little grass. Peoples' yards are just the dirt ground. Downtown is just minutes from the saguaro forest.

Bugs

In the summer there is the palo verde beetle, which can be as long as someone's hand. They fly low in the air and crash into things and crawl around clumsily. There are tiny mosquitoes, which are not native and did not used to be here. There are poisonous spiders like black widows and brown recluses. There are bright green iridescent bugs. There are many kinds of cockroaches. There are tarantulas but it is rare to see them in the city. There are enormous grasshoppers that overpopulate certain areas. Sometimes when you are walking somewhere there will be dozens of enormous grasshoppers jumping all over the place.

Animals

The desert has animals like coyote, javelina, jackrabbits, mountain lions, and rattlesnakes. In the city there are lizards, mice, lots of birds, some small rodents, and stray dogs. In some neighborhoods stray dogs travel in packs. They pretty much leave people alone, but cats have been known to be attacked and killed.

Art

There is plenty of art. There are many art galleries and lots of public art, both sanctioned and unsanctioned. There is a guy that spray paints stencils of famous characters on the sidewalks and on sides of buildings and bridges and the train track. Some of the characters he has spray-painted are Audrey Hepburn, Max Headroom, and Mr. T. It is easy to know the well-known artists in town.

Music

There is plenty of music. Almost every night of the week there is a local band playing in one of the bars. There is blues and bluegrass and lounge and rock and alt-country and more. Some of the bands tour the U.S. and some tour Europe and some do not tour. It is easy to know the well-known musicians in town.

Bicycles

Many people ride bicycles. There are serious bikers that wear spandex and helmets and have fancy skinny bicycles, and there are casual bikers that have vintage cruisers with baskets and bells. It is not uncommon for someone to only have a bicycle, no car. You must be careful when riding your bike across the trolley tracks on 4th Avenue. It is easy to get your wheel caught.

Trains

Cargo trains come through downtown about 150 times a day. The trains are long and the tracks bisect downtown. It is a bitch to get stuck because of one because then you're stuck for a long time. The trains always blow their whistles a lot while they go through. There is a rumor that the city once complained about the noise and so now the conductors blow their whistles just to be antagonistic. But no one seems to mind. The cars are yellow and say Union Pacific. They look beautiful in front of the mountains, like something someone imagined and painted.

Pinstripes

He wears pants. His pants are blue. He enters the room. She sees his pants. She also sees his shirt. His shirt is blue. His blue shirt is a different blue from his blue pants. His pants are dark blue and his shirt is light blue. He also wears shoes. His shoes are black. There are laces. She sees that he wears a jacket. His jacket is black. It has two pockets. There also may be pinstripes. She will find out whether there are pinstripes.

There are pinstripes.

CONVERSATION

She casually mentions things about her history, particularly about her education. She says things like when I was at blank university, and when I graduated from blank university, and after I got my blank degree in blank. She also casually mentions things about her career. I am working as a blank but I am really a blank. She is afraid that the person with whom she is having a conversation might think she is just a blank, even when she feels sure that the person with whom she is having a conversation is just a blank.

LANGUAGE

She is trying to learn his language. She makes T sounds. They are awkward on her tongue. She makes T sounds. They are awkward.

She approaches his language from a different angle. She makes vowels.

You're giving it too much air, he tells her.

Fine, she says.

She studies textbooks and manuals. She gets tapes.

Guh, she tells him. Goo.

He checks his watch.

There's someplace I need to be, he says.

She does not reply.

She will keep trying to learn his language. She will force her mouth around the shape of it, by God.

Thanksgiving

Thanksgiving dinner was at your house. It was beautiful. There was barely enough room. The table seemed ready to buckle under so much bounty, but the table didn't buckle, didn't even groan or tremble or creak. No one, in fact, so much as broke a glass or dropped a spoon or made an awkward joke. You made things just right. You made things perfect.

Thank you for inviting me to Thanksgiving dinner, for including me, poor me, who would probably have been alone otherwise, at home in my pajamas, crying, chewing sloppily on raw carrots, because, as you know, I have no friends and can barely dress myself, and I certainly don't know, anymore, how to eat.

You sat me at the crowded far corner of the table, the furthest from you I could possibly be seated. You were, of course, at the head, tall and handsome, well dressed, the man of the house. You made a toast. You spoke of love and togetherness. You spoke of gratitude. You spoke of God. It was stunning. Everyone ate. I ate only what I could, which was, of course, as always, now, nothing.

I wore, on Thanksgiving Day, my best black dress, and I hoped you wouldn't notice the tattered shoulder straps or the stain on the thigh. I covered my too pale shoulders with a shawl because I am malnourished and am therefore always cold. I covered my thinning hair with my grandmother's black velvet hat, attached to which is a black lace veil, which might have seemed like too much, but at least it covered my terrible face, my mottled skin and dark eyes, and it made it so no one noticed when I looked at you with shameful desire or when my mascara ran. It made it so no one saw when I couldn't swallow any food, when I spat bites discreetly into my napkin. Thank you, darling, for providing me with a napkin. I would never want to embarrass you.

The others at the table fed themselves well, with energy, with concentration, with stamina. It was as if nothing else mattered. There were times during dinner when there was no sound except the sounds of eating: the clattering of forks and spoons, the sawing of knives, the slurping of wine, the busy sounds of breath through the nostrils, the satisfied grunts and burps and mm sounds, the juicy sounds of spit mixing with food mixing with tongues mixing with ripping teeth, the sounds of the mixture being pushed to the backs of the throats and down them, moved along by tight cords of muscle, the food being pushed, shoved, crammed, down down down the throats.

I would look at you during these times. Sometimes you looked back. You knew what I was thinking. You knew how the sounds made me feel. But you wanted me to be strong. So I sat at the table and listened. I smiled when I should have, though it split my dry lips to do so. I took bites and spat them into my receiving napkin. Sometimes, through my black veil, I saw you watch me spit. Then you would take an even bigger bite of food than usual and you would chew and swallow and grunt and raise your glass in celebration. Everyone would join you in a cheer. Everyone would always join you because you were at the head, you were tallest and handsomest, the best dressed, you were the host, you had chosen what would be devoured, or not, and by whom.

This was our arrangement. That I would come. That I would stay. That I would starve. That I would exercise tolerance for, acceptance of, devotion to, that of which I could not partake.

It had been months since I had eaten. Each evening after dark I waited for you to come to my house to feed me. You didn't come, though you always promised that you would. It would always go like this:

I would be in my pajamas lying on my bed and then I would walk to the kitchen. I would pretend that I was about to eat. I would open cabinets and close them. Sometimes I would open and close one cabinet many times in a row. I tried to do it quietly in case you were outside the door, though you never were. I would look at the boxes and bags inside the cabinets, the spices and mixes and cans of things, which were sticky with dust. Sometimes I would say out loud, in a whisper, with my eyes closed, What should we make for dinner tonight? Sometimes I would laugh, in a whisper, at something funny you just said. Sometimes I would stand in front of the sink and pretend that you and I had just finished a big satisfying meal and that I was doing dishes and you were just in the next room digesting and then you would come in the kitchen and you would stand behind me as I washed the dishes and then you would put your hands around my healthy meaty waist and say Thank you for making dinner and for doing the dishes and I would close my eyes and nod and then I would stretch my neck to the side and then you would kiss my neck and the warm water from the faucet would pour over my hands and I would feel loved and settled and satisfied.

But then I would open my eyes. There would be just the running water and the bare sink and my small pale veiny hands and cracked fingernails. There would be my hunched shoulders, my hanging head. I would turn off the water. I would go into the bathroom and turn on the light. I would stare into the mirror. I would pray for you to come, and you never did, you never did, thank God, you never did. I would look gray and starched and terrible. I would look ravaged, ruined, like I loved you, like the way I was meant to love you, like the way you were meant to be loved, like the way you deserved, like I loved you correctly, which I did, oh, I did, my failing hair, my cracked fingernails, oh, I did.

After dinner, everyone at the table bathed you in compliments. They said you were a magician, a wizard, a sorcerer. Their bellies protruded from their trousers. They unbuttoned their buttons. They leaned back in their chairs. They couldn't eat another bite, they said. They said they were stuffed, bloated, full to bursting. Somebody stick a fork in us, they said. We are done. I looked at you at the head of the table, through my black veil, as you received your compliments. You sat up straight, your ears splayed back, listening, receiving, and you graciously, modestly, smiled, nodded, shook your head, lowered your eyes. How good they made you feel. How adored. How gracefully you took it all in. There were smoke breaks, espresso, aperitifs. People got up from their chairs, stretched, walked, conversed, laughed, sat back down, sat on each others' laps. What fun they were having. What celebration. I sipped from a dry teacup. No one talked to me. You were the only one I knew. I looked at you across the room, but you were too busy to look back. You were singing or dancing or telling jokes. You were refilling glasses of wine. You were giving all the people what they wanted. You always gave all the people what they wanted. You never gave me what I wanted, though you always promised that you would, and I believed you. I waited. I hovered. I trembled.

I hung suspended inside my clothes, devoted, starving, hoping, wanting.

But sometimes I doubted you. Sometimes I thought that you were arrogant. Sometimes I thought that you were too tall. Sometimes I thought that you were making a fool out of me, that I was stupid, gullible, that I was being made into a fool.

After a while, a woman (one of your many beautiful woman friends, much more beautiful than me, more beautiful even than the me I was before, who was, in fact, once, actually, if you could believe it to look at me now, rather beautiful) went to the kitchen and brought out the dessert. She brought out pies. There were so many pies. There was apple, pumpkin, blueberry, lemon meringue. There was mincemeat and savory with vegetables. There was chocolate. There was cherry. There were pies with fluffy whipped white clouds and pies with intricate designs on the tops. There were pies dusted with cocoa dust and pies with whole red strawberries. The beautiful woman spread the pies out on the table. Everyone gathered around. Everyone oohed and ahhed and leaned forward and rubbed their hands together.

I stared at the pies. They were beautiful. I held my breath. Behind my black veil, my mouth watered and my eyes dripped. My lips trembled. I could feel my heart beating in my dry throat. I looked at you. You were juggling pies. A cherry and a lemon. I looked back at the pies on the table. I shook inside my black dress. I felt excited and afraid. I felt hungry. I felt afraid of what I might do.

(I couldn't do it, could I? I couldn't possibly. Oh, but suddenly, I confess it, I wanted to. I wanted to more than anything. I wanted to so badly it was as if it was not me who was wanting to. It was something outside of me, behind me, a memory pushing me, an anger, an urgency, a terrible, shameful force.)

(I wanted to do what I was not supposed to do. I wanted to pick up a fork. I wanted to use the side of it to cut. I wanted, then, to turn the fork so that the points were pointing downward. I wanted to push the points into something forgiving. ((Banana cream? Strawberry rhubarb? Huckleberry? Peach?)) I wanted to turn the fork back around in my hand. I wanted to use my arm to raise the fork and bring it toward my face. I wanted to separate my lips. I wanted to guide it in. I wanted to use my lips to pull it off the fork.)

(No. I wanted to use my hands. I wanted to reach into the center of the pie, to the good part, the indelicate part, I wanted to reach into the heart of the pie, to pierce through the outer beautiful skein, to get to the center of it, the nucleus, the wetness, I wanted to touch what made it what it really was, and I wanted to grab it, make a fist, put it in my mouth, and I wanted to use my teeth to chew it, I wanted to use my tongue, I wanted to taste it, to feel it, to wreck it, to make it mine, and I wanted, I wanted, to swallow. ((I wanted for you to see me do it. I wanted for you to see me. I wanted, I confess it (((the shame, the sorrow))) I wanted, for a moment, to make you suffer.))) (I wanted to defy you.)

(I wanted to not disappear.)

Next to the beautiful woman was a stack of small white porcelain plates and a pile of gold forks and a big pie cutter with a heavy ornate handle. The beautiful woman took the big pie cutter with the heavy ornate handle into her strong beautiful hand. She reached her beautiful strong gold arm forward. Beautiful gold bracelets dangled from her thick ornate wrist. She touched the blade of the thick strong pie cutter to the white center of one of the beautiful ornate pies. The porcelain muscles in her strong heavy woman forearm tightened. Her white ornate shoulder rolled forward. She pushed. The thick blade of the pie cutter cut through the beautiful crust and sank into the gold innards of the heavy ornate pie. There was a great holler from the crowd. Steam burst from the pie, and light, and sugar, and chocolate dust, and berries, and a million little stars, and plump, healthy, happy, flying angel babies, and whipped cream, and the bright, promising, perfect future. We all sang, and were thankful. I shut my red eyes. I shut them and opened them.

The beautiful woman loaded the small white porcelain plates with generous, enormous, bursting, heavy slices of pie. She passed them down the table. We dispersed the slices of pie by passing them onto the person next to us, everyone in cooperation, passing, so that there was a choo-choo train of pies around the table, and the pies in the middle of the table were the Christmas village around which the choo-choo train chugged, and the tall people at the table were the pretty snowy mountains, and the people at the ends of the table were the darling bends in the road, and each person who received his or her slice of pie were the adorable red train station with a pointed roof, and the engineer, wearing a blue and white pinstriped cap would lean off the balcony of the train and call out, Everybody off! Last stop! and the people would get their trunks, pick up a fork, eat their pie, close their eyes, and get home safely to the snowmen, and the smoking chimneys, and the brick paths, and the hearth.

And then it was my turn. Everyone but me had their slices of pie. There was one small white porcelain plate left, which was for me, and one gold fork. I looked at the beautiful woman expectantly, and she looked back. She smiled at me, and winked. She began to reach her thick arm forward, her dangling bracelets, her tensing muscles, to cut a piece of pie (for me! for me!) and then my piece of pie was on the ornate pie cutter, and then it was above the small porcelain plate, and then it was sliding off the ornate pie cutter toward the small porcelain plate, the plate, my plate, and then, without warning (I should have known I am so stupid I lost myself I'm sorry) there was a great movement across the table, and it was you (you you you) and you snatched the plate from beneath my sliding melting dripping horrible putrid piece of perfect pie, and you ate my plate.

You ate my plate. You ate it. You crunched it. You shoved it in. You crunched it and crunched it. You crunched every last bit of it. You crunched every last bit of my plate.

Everyone stopped. They watched you. They couldn't believe it. They were aghast. They watched your face twist, your teeth bare themselves, your lips stretch, your eyes squeeze shut. They heard the sounds of your enamel against the porcelain, smashing it, splintering it, grinding it, turning it back to sand, churning it with your spit, squeezing it with your muscles, the sounds of your undoing it, swallowing it, making it disappear, returning my plate to whence it came, to particles, to fluid, to the cells of which we are comprised, to breath, to memory, to the time before we were born, to the planet that harbors us, to outer space, to blackness, to blindness, to our knees, to God, to love.

You struggled at it, of course. You labored. You sweat. You bled. You worked so hard, my darling. I could see that it hurt you. The way the blood dripped down your chin. The way your eyes teared and poured. The way you drooled. The way you whimpered. It was unbecoming, terrible, and yet the most miraculous act I have ever witnessed. How devoted you are. How absolutely passionate. How unshakably correct. How stupid I had been, and now, how ashamed.

When it was over, the beautiful woman handed you a napkin. You sat back down in your chair. You dabbed the blood from your chin, your neck, your collar. You cleared your throat. You cleared it again. We waited for you to collect yourself. Someone poured you a fresh glass of wine. Someone said a prayer. They said:

How we sacrifice.

Everyone took up their glasses and held them – wine dripping sacrificially over their wrists and arms – silently, reverently, in the air. And though I shook, though I struggled, though I was overcome, I wanted to pray too, to pray at the church of you, and so, slowly, laboriously, I also lifted my glass, which was (Semper fidelis nec esuritio effugere quisquam nec amorem potest forever and ever amen) empty.

A Man of Regret

Nice pinstripes, I said to the man at the holiday party who was wearing a suit. It was late in the evening. Things were emptying out. He invited me to the porch for a smoke and I accepted, though our breath came in pale puffs and my thin sleeves were hardly enough to protect me. He sat down on the steps. It was heavy sitting. It wasn't his house. His nose was very pink. He talked real estate, a subject I know nothing about. He confessed everything under his wet towel of retrospect. He should have bought in his twenties when the market was ripe for a rise. You seem like a man of regret, I told him. Oh I am, he said, staring away at something, the other neighborhood steps, the winter cars, the night, his own crystal breathing. He shook his head. Don't make the same mistakes I've made, he said. Buy now. Buy quickly. I understood. I have often wanted to buy. Just last week I saw a set of gold-stemmed martini glasses in a shop window and simply walked on past. And later that day a hot pair of cowboy boots. Waste. I've been thinking of cocktail parties and cattle drives ever since. He slumped over on the steps and after moments of his unmoving I hauled him up. It's not too late, I encouraged him, rattling his shoulder. You could still buy. No, he said sadly. Things wouldn't be the way they might have been. Above our heads icicles sharpened the lining of the house. I quit my rattling. He was probably right. Ten years ago I might have worn those boots with a miniskirt but it didn't occur to me at the time. And now my legs are thicker and I have since lost that sort of edge. Strands of lights everywhere were being switched off. My toes were growing numb and my ankles ached from standing around. He looked terrible. I blamed it all on him. Nice shoes, I barked. They're Italian, he said. They're untied, I told him. He used the side of the house to push himself forward. He looked at his feet. Oh yes, he said breathing heavily. So they are.

WHO WILL TAKE THE CAT

It should be her because the cat wasn't his idea to begin with. It should be him because he named it. She never liked that name anyway. It should be her because it sleeps by her head. It should be him because he gives it a scoop of wet food at dinner. It should be her because she paid for its rabies shots, doesn't he remember, she paid for everything. But wait a second, this whole thing is her fault, who cheated on who, and anyway, it should be him because it sleeps on his lap while he reads. It should be her because he gets to sit home and read since he hasn't had a job in months. It should be him because it lets him rub its belly, that means it trusts him. It should be her because she made up that song about it. It should be him because he named it. He said that already and if he wants to get down to it, it should be her because anyone can see she loves it more. Oh, now she wants to talk about love.

THE WORLD

When you left you said it was not because you did not love me but because you no longer loved where we lived – hated it, in fact – and that you had to travel the world for a while, to gather yourself. I set you free, which was the right thing to do, and I was very strong about it all but in the meantime was experiencing a constant ache, a feeling that my neck and chest were stretching forward with nowhere to go. You sent a letter from somewhere in South America. You wrote that you had climbed a volcano. You said it was amazing. I immediately hated that volcano but made myself be happy for you, which was easier to do by the end of the letter when it said that you broke your toe.

RECORD

What has happened to you in the last three weeks is this:

your girlfriend moved to New York City
your band broke up
your friend died
you started living in your van
you began working more than you are used to.

And so you came to me, of course, and of course I laid myself down
and I was healthy for you, stable, I'm sure, soothing. I have this job
I go to. I have this bed. I have this wine habit and this shower and
these dishes and the way I sing happily to old pop music, the way I
unsleeve records and then sleeve them again, unsleeve them, then
sleeve them. I have this way about me that accepts broken things,
sees they are not broken, tells them they are not broken, and then,
eventually, miraculously, with any luck, they are not broken. I just
sit here. You want to come to me again, come already. This is what
I will, of course, say:

you are not broken
you are not broken
you are not broken
you are not broken
you are not broken, etc.

Woods

When I leave he will live alone in the house in the woods. Each night he will sit on the porch and drink beer in cans. He will smoke cigarettes. He will think about things. I don't know what things he will think about. He will hear sounds. I don't know what sounds he will hear. He will get the heavy silver flashlight and he will shine light into the trees. Sometimes he will see raccoons. Sometimes he will call out to them. He will say taunting things. He will hear his own voice and then he will hear quiet. The quiet he hears will be more quiet after hearing his own voice. He will not get tired until it is very late and then he will try to go to sleep. He will lie down in his underwear. One leg will be on top of the covers. He will close his eyes. He will see colors. I don't know what colors he will see. The window will be open. He will smell the air. I don't know what the air will smell like. If he sleeps he might dream. I don't know what he will dream about. If I lived in the woods I would be a wolf. I would be strong. I would circle the house all night and stay hidden. I would not howl. I would stay close to the ground. If I had to I would fight bears and mountain lions. I would fight other wolves. I would fight men. I would protect the house with him in it. I would keep hurting things away.

The White Cat

It was winter, and nighttime. I was driving to a friend's house in upstate New York. There was a white cat on the side of the road. It had been hit by a car. I pulled over. I kept the headlights on it. It made these movements. It jerked then relaxed then jerked then curled itself up like it was going to sleep. It curled its tail around itself, like it was sleeping in some peaceful place. But it wasn't sleeping. It was dying. It was trying to keep warm, trying to comfort itself. And then it would jerk again. Its white tail would fly upward then come back down.

The friend whose house I was driving to was not a friend I knew very well or liked very much. She and her new husband had just bought this new house and it was all they talked about: bathroom fixtures, cabinetry, redoing the hardwood floors. They were nice people and they had been generous with invitations and dinners and wine. But it was too long a drive to get there for what it was, especially on a northeastern winter night when everything is cold and dark and the car always sputters and stalls and seems like it might not make it.

(My car was always doing that. I was too poor to get a better one. I was much too poor to buy cabinetry, bathroom fixtures, too stupid and lazy to redo a hardwood floor. Much much too unattractive and bitter and drunk to get a nice generous new husband. Better, much better, to stick with men who are poorer, stupider, lazier even than me, who are those things but are also more attractive than me, crazier, drunker, and more talented, maybe even already married, like you, who I loved, oh, I loved you.)

I watched the white cat dying in the headlights for twenty minutes or more. I did not get out of my car. People drove past and swerved.

No one stopped. I kept the white cat in the headlights to protect it from getting hit again. But maybe I shouldn't have. Maybe I should have let it get hit again sooner, to end it, to allow for a quicker end, to allow its puffy white tail to stop its jerking and flailing, to allow a careless vehicle to come and make its neck stop stretching, to make its eyes stop looking, to make it so it didn't feel so cold and alone, dying all by itself in the winter at night on pavement.

When I got to my friend's house I told her and her husband about the white cat. They poured me a glass of wine and gave me food and listened. They tried to comfort me with vague cliched phrases like "time to die," "not in pain anymore," and "in a better place." There was a fire in their new gas fire area and their new kitchen was warm and cheerful even with the few remaining rough unfinished edges. I smiled and nodded and drank their wine but did not eat their food. I spoke in their language in order to agree with them, to end it, so they would feel like they had been wise and successful, so they would feel like they had been soothing to sensitive little me.

(I reject comfort. I do not do things that are good ideas. I use poor judgment. I seek difficult or impossible situations in which to put myself and when difficult or impossible situations do not exist, I create them. I say no to offers of good things from good people and I say yes when someone offers me something bad. When something breaks I do not fix it nor do I dispose of its pieces. I bring the pieces to bed with me night after night after night, I hold them, I dream of you, I miss you, I would have continued to accept anything, you are good, you are, I cup my red hands to balance you in them, I offer you your exquisite reflection.)

I called the cops from my car while I watched the white cat dying in the headlights. The cops didn't care, as I knew they wouldn't, though they wouldn't admit they didn't care, instead they made up some excuse about not having enough cops on duty that night in that area at that time. I cried to the woman on the phone. I told her about the white cat. I described its flailing jerking tail, its opening and shutting eyes, how it kept curling around itself in an attempt at sleep and warmth and finishing. The woman listened, was sympathetic but firm, and I knew, I knew, I sounded like a crazy person, lost, inappropriate, misguided, a bleeding heart. Just a cat, she didn't say but said. Just a cat, said the cars, swerving to avoid us.

The white cat jerked, flailed, attempted sleep, its tail flew up and came back down, it didn't die and didn't die and didn't die. It was so cold that night, the kind of cold that makes everything, the ground, the air, the trees, tense and mean and brittle.

(I ask for help from the wrong sources at the wrong time. I usually ask for help after I have already done something terribly wrong, when I have gotten in too deep, when I have turned my nose up at a banquet of good advice. No wonder they are disgusted. No wonder they are fed up. I am fed up. I am disgusted. And all I have, now, is you, because you know, because you messed it up along with me, but I don't have you, maybe I never did, I see your eyes now and they are decided, they tell me back away, so I'm backing, because I do what you tell me to, that's how I was trained, and I curl up now under blankets and remember when I was allowed to come near you, near you, because I gave up all others for you, for you, because you are perfect, because I believed, like a child, that sacrifice would lead me to heaven.)

I had drunk too much wine at my friend's house with not enough food, no food, in fact, and I started, I guess, to look distant, as if I were, perhaps, thinking. What's wrong? they asked, and I told them the white cat. I told them I could not stop seeing it there in my headlights, dying. I remember that they looked at me tenderly but that their asses gave them away, shifting around in their chairs uncomfortably, pitying me. They had already said their piece, had already given me what adages they had saved for the subject of unfortunate untimely violent animal death, and it was, clearly, annoying, that I was still attached, stuck, harping, hadn't by now, for God's sake this again, moved on.

(I am always the sucker. I have always been. As a child I always wanted to play orphan, fire, flood, any scene having to do with suffering, with emergency, (and finally, with deliverance), and I always felt it, believed it, became emotional, and my friends, then, found it un-fun, and I would, then, have to back off, break out the Barbies, lighten it up, so that they wouldn't leave. Too much, I am. Too much. I am sorry for my company. I am sorry how much I worry, how much I want. I am sorry I say what I mean. I am sorry I didn't know it was playtime for you, sorry I took you seriously, sorry I carried your words home with me, held them, petted them, thanked them for coming into this world, for being propelled by life, sorry I got familiar with your hair, your face, your hands, sorry I thought I was back home at Christmas when really I was lighting the last matches on the street corner, freezing to death. I shouldn't have. (God then delivered me. I went into the light.))

I did not go to it. I did not get out. It would have been cold, poor me, it would have been scary. It would have been embarrassing, all those cars, swerving, seeing me do it, seeing me try. The white cat might have been angry if I attempted a rescue, it might have spat at me, bit me, hissed, told me to leave it the hell alone, dying, thanks, I'm dying, and I don't even know you.

I didn't want, ultimately, I guess, maybe, (or maybe something else), to interrupt. What had happened already, had happened.

(I touched your stomach once and I felt, finally, like the time had come for me to receive what I had, tirelessly, hoped for, what I had, tirelessly, worked for, what I had expected to come from enough tireless hope, enough tireless silence. This, I suppose, is my misfortune, my incapability, my pathetic miscarriage, my lesson, my failed attempt to do good, be good, my confusion about, and my dependency upon, that meaningless word, which, I thought, once upon a time, meant that I should do nothing.)

I left my friend's house. I said my goodbyes and I said them politely, graciously. I complimented them on what needed complimenting. I thanked them. I put my coat on with delicate humility. I got back in my car. I took a different route home so that I would not see the white cat, so that I would not see what I had not done.

(Or maybe I could have been braver, smarter, more determined. Maybe I could have scooped it up from the pavement, petted it, said the words that would have come through me from God. Maybe the warmth of my arms would have been enough. Maybe the press of my chest. Maybe I would have driven like a demon with it in my lap all the way to the ER, maybe I would have had enough money, maybe it would have been the right doctor. Maybe I would have celebrated in the waiting room. Maybe I would have brought it home, lived the rest of my life looking, amazed, at this being. I would have named it. I would have held it. It would have been soft, gentle, warm, healthy, eating, rubbing its face on corners, sleeping under blankets, and maybe I would have thought, each time it stepped, stretched, yawned, breathed: I saved you.)

CHICKENS

She is driving behind a truck on the highway. She moves into the right lane to pass the truck. She watches the truck on the left as she passes. The truck is full of chickens. There are hundreds of chickens. The chickens are stuffed in the truck. The white feathers of the chickens rattle in the wind of the highway. She can see their faces. There are chickens on the inside that she cannot see. The chickens are closed in together. The chickens are pushed into small boxes. The small boxes are piled box on box on box. She is moving quickly on the highway. Everything is confusing. She approaches the cab of the truck. There is a man driving the truck. She rolls down her window and sticks out her head. Her hair gets in her face. The man driving the truck smiles at her and looks back at the road and smiles at her and looks back at the road. The chickens, she yells, and the words get lost on the highway, fly backward, hit pavement, roll. The man smiles at her and gives her thumbs up. The chickens, she yells again, and the man blows her a kiss. She looks at all the chickens. She looks at all the chickens. It is dangerous on the highway. She looks straight out her windshield. It is dangerous everywhere. She picks up speed and she passes the truck of chickens.

PORTRAIT

My grandmother's house was a New England farmhouse that was built by her father. My grandmother was born in the kitchen. It was quiet inside the house, and dark, mostly dark anyway, dark inside the front hall. The door was never locked. My grandmother did not hear well. My father would open the door and we would enter the hall. The old clock would be ticking. My father would say Mother Mother We're here, and I could see the back of my grandmother's head from over the top of her armchair in the living room slowly turn around. The front hall had a long dark red carpet and heavy oak furniture and on the wall was a huge portrait in a heavy frame. It was of a large man with a black beard and black robes holding a black book, his right hand raised. I believed that the man was God and I was small and would walk carefully past Him. Sometimes after dinner I would challenge myself to enter the front hall alone, to tiptoe, trembling, to stand in front of God, to look at Him, to keep standing, to keep looking, to stand looking, unafraid, at God.

HEAVEN

I read once that in heaven you are the age you were in life when you first recognized your own death. When I was six I sunk into a vision in which I was buried and dead and people who were alive walked on the grass above me. In this vision I saw the people's feet and I saw the grass. It was a beautiful sunny day. The grass was green. A woman walked above me in a knee-length skirt and heels.

If the person who wrote what I read is correct, if I understood correctly what I read, if I am remembering correctly what I understood, if I am remembering correctly that I had this vision when I was six, if I am remembering this vision correctly, if it was a vision, if this vision is an indication that I recognized my own death, if there is a heaven, if I go to heaven, then in heaven I will be six.

JUMP

I was often scared at night. I imagined fires and tried to think of ways to save my family. Would we survive jumping. My cat Whimsy used to get in bed with me and lick my forehead until my forehead was very soft. I would hold Whimsy when I jumped. I would be careful not to crush her. I would position myself to land on my feet or on my back.

TRUNK

An old woman in my village lived in a big Victorian house with many cats. One night the old woman's house was on fire. People stood watching. Cats ran out flaming. There were around forty cats. The old woman was saved. The day after the fire I rode my bike over and stood on the gravel. I could see inside the house. Everything was black. There were spaces that had been rooms. There were piles that had been things. There were no cats anywhere. One man stood on the burnt out second floor. One man stood on the ground. A wooden trunk was being lowered on a rope.

Recess

A girl I knew at school had a brother who smashed her rabbit's head in with a brick. The girl wanted to be friends. I saw the girl in the park once with her mother. The girl's mother was drunk and wailing with bleeding fingers. I was then thereafter scared of the girl. A boy in my class at recess said if you like Maria raise your hand. Maria looked at me terrified. I was the only one who might have. I didn't.

Poor bunny

DOCTOR

I am standing on the porch of my house in the woods. It is night.
I hear things in the woods. I shine a flashlight. Nothing but trees
and wind and sound. I turn and shine the flashlight at my house.
My house is covered in blankets quilts and tapestries. They catch
the wind. They shiver and blow. A woman appears on the steps. I
shine my flashlight. The woman is wearing skirts and jewelry and
a scarf around her head. She is cradling a dog. The dog is frail and
thin. We need a doctor, the woman says. I look into the woods
behind the woman. In the dark I can see a carriage in the woods. I
can see children. There are many children. They are barefoot and
have long dirty yellow hair. The children squat on the ground and
pull up grass and leaves. There are bears in the woods. There are
mountain lions and wolves. I am worried about the children. We
need a doctor, the woman says. I look at the dog. I know there is
a doctor somewhere close but I can't remember how to find him.

pon ellos

Village

I am driving on a road in the woods at night. There are no houses anywhere. I round a bend and a deer comes leaping from the woods. I hit the deer. I get out of the car. The deer is dead. The car is ruined. I am stranded and afraid. I know there is a village nearby but it is too far to walk. I need the dead deer to carry me to the village. I lift the dead deer and straddle its back. The dead deer is heavy and does not respond. Its head droops. I hold the dead deer up. I walk a few feet holding the dead deer up beneath me. I hold the dead deer up by placing one hand beneath its belly and one hand beneath its neck. The dead deer's hooves drag on the pavement as I walk. It is the only sound. The dead deer is warm and soft. It is a slow effort for both of us.

Cow

She visits a farm in southern New Hampshire. It is a small farm. In the morning she goes to the barn. Next to the barn are two little houses like doghouses. They are houses for young boy cows. There is a young boy cow in one of the houses. She approaches the young boy cow and offers her hand. The young boy cow licks her hand. His tongue is thick and pink and very soft. His eyes are soft and so is his hair. In one half hour from the moment the young boy cow licks her hand he will be led from the little house and put on a truck. The truck will take him to a bigger farm in southern New Hampshire where he will be killed. It will be a forty-five minute drive to the bigger farm. The truck will take him through many miles of countryside and mountains and will run past people's houses. The road will be bumpy in places. The driver of the truck will stop for lunch. He will have egg salad and a Coke. He will eat his lunch in the truck. There will be seven total stoplights. The air will smell like apple blossoms. At the bigger farm it will be three and one half hours before the young boy cow is killed. Killing him will take a certain amount of time. Certain things will happen. He will make certain noises.

HORSE

There is a war happening in another country. There are horses that are native to the other country where the war is. The horses are not regular horses. They are very big and muscular and they have charcoal colored skin instead of hair. She can see the horses. They have enormous teeth that are long and pointed. The horses are endangered in the country where the war is. There is a soldier who is specially trained to kill the horses that are endangered in the country where the war is. She can see the soldier. The horses line up in pairs before the soldier. The pair of horses in the front of the line charges the soldier. She can see the horses' charcoal skin and their muscles as they run toward the soldier, and the horses show their long enormous pointed teeth. The soldier crouches on the ground and waits for the horses. When the horses are close to the soldier, the soldier springs from the ground and brings a large watermelon down upon the horses' heads. The horses are then stunned and wounded. The soldier then uses a long pointed blade to halve the horses' heads. The horses fall dead. The soldier then returns to his position and crouches on the ground and waits for the next pair of horses. The next pair of horses charges the soldier and the soldier springs from the ground and brings a large watermelon down upon the horses' heads. The horses are then stunned and wounded. The soldier then uses a long pointed blade to halve the horses' heads. The horses fall dead. The soldier then returns to his position and crouches on the ground and waits for the next pair of horses. This will continue until the soldier who is specially trained to kill the horses has killed all the horses. The horses will continue to line up in pairs and to charge the soldier and to be killed.

Opossum

Each day she drives to her job. She passes the airport. One morning when she passes the airport there is a dead opossum in the road. The opossum is whole on one side and is bloody and smeared on the other. She swerves her car to avoid the opossum. She tries to send the opossum up to God. She thinks hard as she drives about sending the opossum up to God. She tries to think the opossum upward, but her thinking is trapped in her skull and does not reach the opossum and does not reach God. She breathes deeply and tries to feel in her shoulders and in the back of her neck and to make this feeling reach the opossum and to make this feeling reach God, but this feeling is trapped within the words contained in her skull such as Please, God, take the opossum, and Opossum, go on up to God. She cannot rid herself of the words. The words do not reach the opossum and the words do not reach God.

por possum

ACKNOWLEDGEMENTS

Many thanks to the editors of the following journals, in which sections of *The State of Kansas* have appeared:

"The White Cat," *Caketrain* 5
"The State of Kansas," *Cranky* V1n3
"Conversation," *Cranky* V1n2
"Thanksgiving," *Denver Quarterly* V44n2
"The Body," *Folio* Winter 2004
"A Man of Regret" and "Who Will Take the Cat," *Gargoyle* 50
"Record," *Gargoyle* 52
"Chickens," "Dog," and "Opposum," *Harness Magazine* V2n2
"Neighborhood," *In Posse Review* 24
"Business Idea," "Home," and "Your Maid in Real Life," *No Contest*
"Pretend," *Tarpaulin Sky* V1n1
"A Brief Introduction to Downtown Tucson," *Trickhouse* V1

Many special thanks to Michael Boyko, Ruth Adams Bronz, Michael Costello, Barbara DeCesare, Ellen Fladger, Elena Georgiou, Maggie Golston, Annie Guthrie, Ruby Jets, Alicia Keenan, Kristi Maxwell, Kristen Nelson, Christian Peet, Vic Perry, Noah Saterstrom, Selah Saterstrom, Travis Smith, Scott Wheeler, and Becca Whitehead for, at various critical moments, being my readers, editors, and visionaries; to Geralee Hall, Noah Saterstrom, and Jenn Morrison Whittingham, whose artwork helped shape this project; and to my teachers, Rebecca Brown, Jan Clausen, Harry Marten, Jim McCord, and Jordan Smith; to the real-life cottage girls; and to my family.

About the Author

Julianna Spallholz has collaborated and performed her short and very short fiction with musicians, visual artists, a DJ, and a chef. She teaches writing and English in upstate New York and is at work on a second collection of short fictions. *The State of Kansas* is her debut collection.

Available from GenPop Books

Judith Baumel, *The Kangaroo Girl*
Emma Bolden, *Malificae*
Michael Klein, *then, we were still living*
John Philpin, *Bad Dog*
Julianna Spallholz, *The State of Kansas*
Alan Semerdjian, *In the Architecture of Bone*

& the online magazine from GenPop Books:
No Contest

www.genpopbooks.com